Teacher's Pet

Elizabeth could hardly wait to tell her mother the news. "Mom, it's getting exciting! Madame André told us about the audition next Saturday for the recital. Isn't it exciting, Jessica?"

"How could it be exciting for me?" Jessica retorted. "Madame André doesn't like me. She only likes you."

"That' not true," said Elizabeth.

"It is so, and you know it!" cried Jessica angrily. "Madame never even looks at me."

Elizabeth looked shocked. "Jessica, you're wrong. Madame André knows what a wonderful dancer you are."

I'm sure that's true," said Mrs. Wakefield. "You're both such good dancers. Madame André must be thrilled to have the two of you in her class."

Jessica didn't answer. It was bad enough that Elizabeth was teacher's pet. Now her own mother was taking sides against her!

SWEET VALLEY TWINS

Teacher's Pet

Written by
Jamie Suzanne

Created by
FRANCINE PASCAL

A BANTAM SKYLARK BOOK®
TORONTO · NEW YORK · LONDON · SYDNEY · AUCKLAND

RL 4, 008–012

TEACHER'S PET

A Bantam Skylark Book / September 1986

Skylark Books is a registered trademark of Bantam Books, Inc.
Registered in U.S. Patent and Trademark Office and elsewhere.

Sweet Valley High and Sweet Valley Twins are trademarks of Francine Pascal

Conceived by Francine Pascal

Produced by Cloverdale Press Inc.

Cover art by James Mathewuse

ISBN 0-553-15422-2

Published simultaneously in the United States and Canada

Bantam Books are published by Bantam Books, Inc. Its trade-
mark, consisting of the words "Bantam Books" and the por-
trayal of a rooster, is Registered in U.S. Patent and Trademark
Office and in other countries. Marca Registrada. Bantam
Books, Inc., 666 Fifth Avenue, New York, New York 10103.

PRINTED IN THE UNITED STATES OF AMERICA

O   0 9 8 7 6 5 4 3 2 1

For Rebecca Quaretti-Lee

One

◇

"Practice, practice, practice! That's all Madame André ever thinks about. Doesn't she know I practice night and day as it is? Why do I have to ruin a perfectly good Saturday by going to another ballet class?"

Jessica Wakefield stood in the middle of the practice area she and her twin sister Elizabeth had set up in the basement. Her blue-green eyes, which looked dazzling when she was happy, had lost their sparkle. Madame André, the twins' dance instructor, had just phoned and asked them to come to her studio.

Elizabeth was on the floor doing her stretching exercises. She looked up at her sister's sad expression. She sighed. "Oh, Jess, it won't be so bad. It's just for a couple of hours. Besides, you love to dance."

It was true. Elizabeth often grew tired of practicing the hour a day that Madame had recommended. But Jessica sometimes practiced for two full hours. Still, Elizabeth knew that Jessica hated to change her plans with her friends for anyone or anything.

Even though the two sixth-grade girls both had long blond hair that glinted in the sunlight, aquamarine eyes, and tiny dimples in each left cheek, they were really very different. Jessica liked to talk about boys and clothes, and always wanted to have as much fun as possible. Elizabeth liked more serious things—reading and writing and long talks with a good friend. Elizabeth was four minutes older than Jessica. She wondered if that was why she could handle Madame André's sudden Saturday practice more calmly than her sister.

"Well, you would think that Madame André would notice how good I am," Jessica protested. "But, no. She's never looking when I do a perfect pirouette. She's too busy looking at you and telling the entire class how wonderful you are and how beautifully you dance. And now this! Lila Fowler and I and all the other Unicorns had such important plans for today."

Jessica bit her lower lip. She shouldn't have said anything about her plans with Lila Fowler and the Unicorns. After all, she really wanted to dance the part of Swanilda in the upcoming recital. Besides, she knew Elizabeth didn't like the Unicorns.

"How can your plans with the Unicorns be as exciting as going to ballet class? Today we'll find out about the audition for the fall recital. You know how much you want the lead."

Jessica thought for a moment. She was determined to get the part of Swanilda, no matter what. She would prove to Madame that she was the best dancer in the class, better even than her sister. But why had Madame called the practice for this afternoon?

The day before, Jessica had overheard Bruce Patman and some of his friends discussing plans to go surfing. She told Lila and the other girls in the club that the boys would be at the beach today. Then they had planned to ride their bikes to the beach and spend the afternoon watching them surf.

"Of course I'll go to practice," said Jessica, trying not to sound angry. "Even though I promised the Unicorns that I'd go to the beach with them. They'll probably think that I don't keep my promises."

Elizabeth glanced at her watch. "You'd better hurry. We need to leave for the Dance Studio in fifteen minutes. I'll go on up and change."

Elizabeth raced up the basement stairs and into the comfortable den of the Wakefields' roomy split-level house. She paused and listened for a moment to be sure that Jessica was coming upstairs, too. Then she hurried into the kitchen to get a drink of water before she went on up to her room. She felt a rush of happiness as she stepped into the bedroom. Just recently it had been transformed from a guest room into her own private room. Elizabeth had helped decorate it herself and had picked the cream-colored paint for the walls and the navy blue bedspread and curtains with bright yellow accents. Still, she sometimes missed the pink and white room that she had shared with Jessica. She remembered the whispered conversations the two of them used to have at night after the lights went out. Jessica kept the other room now.

As Elizabeth put her leotard, tights, and ballet slippers into her dance bag, she smiled. She was very glad that Jessica had decided to stay in ballet class instead of quitting as she had threatened to do a few days before. Elizabeth was glad, too, that Jessica would be spending the day with her instead of going to the beach with the Unicorns. Even though they were beginning to have separate interests, they were identical twins and each other's best friend.

"Elizabeth, are you coming?" Jessica called up from the kitchen. "You know how angry Madame André gets when people are late to class."

Elizabeth smiled to herself and hurried to join her sister. If she hadn't heard it with her own ears, she would never have believed that Jessica was worried about being late. Jessica always seemed to think that nothing ever started until she arrived.

As the girls hurried to the Dance Studio, Elizabeth thought about how much she loved living in Sweet Valley. It was a pretty town, just a short bike ride from the ocean, and the warm California sunshine made it feel like summer almost all year long.

The twins were out of breath when they reached the Dance Studio. They opened the heavy glass doors and waved to Mrs. Hanley, the receptionist. Then they hurried to the changing room.

"Hi, Elizabeth! Hi, Jessica!" Thirteen other sixth-grade girls greeted the twins with excited chatter as they changed into their dance clothes.

"Who do you think will get to dance the solo part in the recital?" asked Jo Morris.

"I'll bet it will be Elizabeth," said Amy Sutton. "Madame is always complimenting her." Amy had just started taking classes a couple of weeks earlier. She loved sports much more than ballet and would rather play soccer or softball than dance any day. But her mother insisted on the ballet lessons. Madame now seemed to spend as much time criticizing Amy as she spent complimenting Elizabeth.

"I think it will be Elizabeth, too," Kerry Glenn added, twirling the long dark braid that hung down her back almost to her waist.

Jessica jerked on her slippers and tried to concentrate on tying up her hair into a ponytail. But she felt hurt by the girls' remarks. Madame André seemed to think that Elizabeth was the star of the class. Now everyone else thought so, too. Well, she would show them if it was the last thing she did.

As soon as everyone was dressed in leotards and tights, they moved in a group to the studio. One by one they glanced nervously at the life-size doll in the chair at the front of the room. That must be Coppelia, Elizabeth thought, the doll in the ballet number that the class was performing for the recital.

Jessica was careful to stay close to Amy Sutton. Maybe Amy's miserable attempts at ballet would make Jessica's dancing look even better. Then Madame would have to notice her and choose her for the lead.

Madame André stood beside the barre as she watched her students enter the studio. She was a tall, thin woman who carried herself as if she were a queen. The class bowed deeply to her, and she returned their bow with a dignified nod of her head.

"Good afternoon, class," she said.

"Good afternoon, Madame André," they answered in unison.

"First position at the barre, *s'il vous plaît*," she told the girls. Her English had a thick French accent.

The girls took their places. They stood with their left sides toward the barre, their left hands resting gently on it, and heels together. Their toes were turned out to form an almost straight line. Just as she had planned, Jessica stood next to Amy.

Madame André led the girls through their barre work. She paced back and forth in front of them, stopping to compliment a student here or criticize one there. But she did not say a word to Jessica.

"Amy, pull in your stomach."

"*Bien,* Elizabeth, what a beautiful plié."

"Tina, get those heels together."

"Amy, you still have a poor turnout. How many times have I told you that without a good turnout, you can never be a good dancer?"

Jessica turned her knees far out over her feet and held her body perfectly erect. She hoped that Madame would see that she had the best turnout in the class.

"Now class. Battement glissé."

At last, thought Jessica. Battement glissé was her favorite step. Madame would have to notice her now.

"Elizabeth! Your battement glissé is almost perfect! Look, class, watch Elizabeth's battement glissé."

"Elizabeth's battement glissé," Jessica muttered under her breath. Elizabeth's wasn't half as good as her own. Why was Madame always complimenting Elizabeth instead of her?

Jessica watched as Elizabeth did another battement glissé. It was OK, she thought sadly, but Elizabeth should have moved more sharply and her foot should have come up off the floor.

Finally the barre work was over. Madame André picked up the life-size doll that was sitting in the chair. She gestured for the class to sit and form a semicircle around her.

"We will skip center practice for today so that we may have time to talk more about the audition and the beautiful ballet you will dance in our fall recital," she said. Her eyes were sparkling. Her face always seemed to shine when she talked about performing onstage.

"As you know, our recital will be held three weeks from Sunday in the auditorium at Sweet Valley High School. We will take our recital number from the beautiful classical ballet *Coppelia*, which is named after this doll. Coppelia was so lifelike that both the heroine, Swanilda, and her true love, Franz, were fooled into thinking she was a real girl. The scene we will be dancing is in the shop of the old dollmaker, Coppelius. In this scene the other dolls he has created have been wound up so that they dance, too. Most of you will be in the corps de ballet, dancing the parts of the village people. But I will be choosing five of you to dance solos. Four of you will have the smaller parts of the dolls. One will dance the lovely solo of Swanilda."

"Oh, Madame André," Elizabeth said dreamily. "I know it's going to be beautiful."

"Yes, Elizabeth," said Madame, smiling softly. "I am going to hold an audition one week from today at three o'clock in the afternoon. I want everyone in the class to dance for me. I will choose the girl for the part of Swanilda and for the other parts."

Jessica, too, has been captured by the romantic story, and she imagined herself whirling across the stage as the beautiful Swanilda. *When I audition all by myself for Madame,* she thought, *she will have to see how well I dance. And then I'll win Swanilda's part.*

"Everyone practice!" Madame called gaily as the girls filed toward the changing room. "Remember, five of you will dance special parts, but only one of you will be Swanilda. That person will have to practice even longer and harder." Then Madame looked directly at Elizabeth. Jessica's hopes faded as Madame's face lit up in a brilliant smile.

Two

◇

Elizabeth could hardly wait to tell her mother the news about the recital. She was glad her mother had planned to pick up the twins after class that day. Elizabeth jumped into the Wakefields' sleek silver and maroon van ahead of Jessica. Before her mother could pull out of the parking lot, Elizabeth began chattering away.

"Mom, it's getting so exciting! Madame André told us about the audition next Saturday for the recital. She said that she wants everyone to dance for her. Five girls will get solos, but Swanilda is still the biggest part. Isn't it exciting, Jessica?"

"How could it be exciting for me?" Jessica retorted. "Madame André doesn't like me. She only
likes you."

"That is not true," said Elizabeth. It hurt her to
think of Jessica saying mean things about someone
as wonderful as Madame André.

"It is so, and you know it!" cried Jessica angrily. Then she became sad and hurt, and tears
filled her eyes. "Oh, Lizzie, you don't know how
terrible it is to be ignored. Madame never looks at
me. She never sees my pliés or battements glissés
because she's always looking at you. You're teacher's pet. You know you are. Madame likes you three
hundred thirty-seven times more than she likes
me!"

Elizabeth looked shocked. "Jessica, you're
wrong," she protested. "Madame André knows
what a wonderful dancer you are. Maybe today was
just an unlucky day for you."

"I'm sure that's true," said Mrs. Wakefield as
she pulled the van to a stop in the driveway. "You're
both such good dancers. Madame André must be
thrilled to have the two of you in her class."

Jessica didn't answer. It was bad enough that
Elizabeth was teacher's pet. Now her own mother
was taking sides against her. She slammed the van

door and hurried into the house. She almost tripped over her brother, Steven, who was sprawled across the den floor watching a football game on TV.

"Watch it, Twinkle-Toes," he called out as she raced past him heading for the stairs. "I thought you were supposed to be learning to be graceful in your ballet class."

Why was everyone being so mean to her today? Jessica wondered. She went upstairs to her bedroom and tossed her dance bag onto the heap of clothing on the floor. She could forgive Steven, she supposed. After all, what did a fourteen-year-old know about ballet, or about how much it hurt to be overlooked by Madame André? But Elizabeth ought to understand.

Jessica thought back to the first day of ballet class. She had wanted to make a good impression on Madame that day, so she'd dressed up in a new purple leotard and purple leg warmers, and pinned her hair back with barrettes that had purple ribbons hanging from them. She'd even put on some makeup so that Madame André would be sure to notice her.

Madame had certainly noticed her. A look of shock had crossed her face when Jessica entered the room. In front of everyone Madame scolded her for showing off. She'd told Jessica that from then on she had to wear simple colors, put her hair up in a bun, and that no makeup was allowed in her studio.

But that was weeks ago, Jessica thought. Surely Madame couldn't hold a grudge for that long! She had no reason to like Elizabeth so much better than her. Besides, dancing the part of Swanilda wouldn't mean nearly as much to Elizabeth.

Elizabeth liked ballet, but she liked writing a lot better. Elizabeth was even in charge of the sixth-grade newspaper, *The Sweet Valley Sixers*. Jessica sighed deeply. Dancing was much more special to her. She didn't just hear the music, she felt it. When she started to dance, she forgot about everything else. It was as though she became part of the music as she whirled around the room.

Jessica gazed into the mirror and pictured herself standing in the center of the stage, ready to begin her solo. Her hair was pulled up onto the top of her head and she was wearing a jeweled crown. Her costume was the most beautiful she had ever seen. It was the exact turquoise of her eyes and had clouds of lace for a skirt. The orchestra had finished the introduction. The first strains of the solo piece floated into the air, and it was time for her to dance.

Her dream was interrupted by a soft knock at her bedroom door. "It's me, Jessica. May I come in?"

It was Elizabeth. What could she want? And why had she picked such a terrible time to want to come in?

"I don't feel like talking right now," said Jessica.

Outside the door, Elizabeth sighed. "Please let me come in, Jess. Please?"

Elizabeth waited for her sister to answer, feeling tears brimming in her eyes. Jessica was the most important person in the whole world to her, and she couldn't let ballet class come between them.

Finally, Jessica opened the door and said that Elizabeth could come inside.

Elizabeth ran to her sister and hugged her. "Oh, Jessica. Everything is going to be OK. I just know it is."

"How could it?" Jessica challenged her sister. "You're teacher's pet, and you always will be. You could fall flat on your face, and she would ask you to do it again as a demonstration for the class."

Elizabeth started to giggle, but the hurt look on Jessica's face changed the giggle to a sigh.

"I've been thinking about this a lot," she said slowly, "and I think the reason Madame never sees how well you dance is because you stand next to Amy Sutton. Amy is really nice and all, but let's face it, she isn't much of a dancer. I think it drives Madame André crazy to see someone dance so poorly."

"But don't you see?" Jessica asked. "Dancing next to Amy makes me look even better."

"I'm not so sure, Jessica. Amy never does anything right and Madame is always criticizing her. I think Madame is so busy looking at Amy that she doesn't notice you."

Jessica looked at her sister and wondered. Could that be true? Maybe dancing next to Amy Sutton was doing her more harm than good.

Elizabeth took a deep breath and went on. "I thought that maybe you and I could start helping Amy. You know, invite her over to practice for the audition together and help her improve her dancing. Then Madame won't be yelling at her so much, and she'll have more time to notice you."

Jessica's face lit up. "Elizabeth Wakefield, you're a genius! Of course we can help Amy."

"Oh, Jessica, I'm so glad you like my idea. Let's invite Amy to come home with us and practice after school Monday."

Jessica nodded, but she'd barely heard what Elizabeth had said. Here was a wonderful chance to impress Madame André. For the first time all day Jessica's eyes sparkled happily. She could just picture Madame André smiling at her and saying, "I did not realize you were so dedicated."

Three

◆

On Monday morning the Unicorns gathered outside on the school steps just as they did almost every day before the bell. Jessica hurried to meet them. The more she thought about impressing Madame André, the more certain she was of getting the solo part she knew she deserved.

"On Saturday Madame André is holding an audition for the big fall recital," she announced as soon as she reached the group. "I just have to get the lead."

The others all stopped their chattering and looked at Jessica.

"I'm sure that nobody else has a chance against you," Lila Fowler said confidently. "After all, you're the only Unicorn in the class. Everybody knows that Unicorns are very pretty and *very* special."

It was the exact reaction that Jessica had hoped for. She smiled, thinking how wonderful it was to have Lila Fowler for a friend. Not only had Lila been the one to get Jessica accepted into the most exclusive club in school, but her father was very rich. *Lila and the other Unicorns will really admire me when I get the solo part*, Jessica thought.

"We'll all go to the recital together," said Ellen Riteman. "And we'll clap louder than anyone when you dance."

Jessica couldn't have been happier. She wanted to keep the conversation going a little longer, but the first bell rang. It was time for class.

"Don't forget the special Unicorn meeting after school," Kimberly Haver called over her shoulder as she took off down the hall.

Jessica nodded, trying briefly to remember what else it was that she had planned to do after school, then dismissed it with a shrug.

Elizabeth hung her jacket inside her locker and pulled out the books for her morning classes. She looked around for Amy. She had been surprised when Jessica had agreed to help Amy with her ballet steps after school. The more she thought about it, the better she felt.

Elizabeth finally got to talk to Amy after lunch, when she went to Mr. Bowman's classroom to turn in an article that she had written for the sixth-grade newspaper. Mr. Bowman was the teacher in charge of the paper, *The Sweet Valley Sixers*, which came out once every two weeks. One corner of his room contained a gray file cabinet, a small desk, and an old manual typewriter, which the newspaper staff used. Amy was sitting at the desk pecking at the keyboard of the typewriter with two fingers.

"Hi, Amy," Elizabeth called as she dropped her story into a basket on the desk. "What are you doing?"

"Oh, hi, Elizabeth. I'm writing an article on the ballet recital and the audition. I asked Mr. Bowman about it, and he liked the idea."

"So do I. I'm glad you thought of it. By the way, I was wondering if you'd like to come home with Jessica and me after school today to practice ballet. It would be lots of fun."

"Gee, thanks. I'd love to come."

"Great!" said Elizabeth. "I'll wait for you at my locker after school."

Elizabeth leaned against her locker after the dismissal bell rang later that afternoon. She wondered where her twin could be, although Jessica was famous for being late. Still, Elizabeth had been so excited about helping Amy that she had just expected her sister to be waiting anxiously beside the locker as well. A moment later Amy came hurrying up.

"I called my mom to tell her I was going to your house. She'll pick me up at four o'clock. She'd do anything to have me become a star ballerina," Amy said with a sigh. "Where's Jessica?" she added, glancing around.

"I don't know," Elizabeth confessed. "But I'm sure she'll be along in a minute. She was really excited about the three of us practicing together."

But ten minutes later Jessica still hadn't shown up, so Amy and Elizabeth decided to go on without her. On the way to the Wakefield house the girls talked about school and working on the sixth-grade paper together. As usual, Elizabeth enjoyed talking to Amy. She was a good friend and the two of them had lots of things in common.

Elizabeth and Jessica had set up a practice area in the basement, turning the overstuffed sofa around so that they could use the back as a barre. As Elizabeth and Amy changed into their practice clothes, they kept listening for Jessica. Elizabeth wondered why she was so late, but still her twin did not appear.

"This is going to be fun," Amy said with a nervous giggle. "Do you have any music?"

"One practice record coming up!" Elizabeth put a record on the turntable and carefully lowered the tone arm. Then she hurried to the back of the sofa and stood behind Amy, waiting for the music to start.

The girls went through the five basic positions and moved on to the more complicated steps. Elizabeth could see at once why Madame was always criticizing Amy. Her movements were jerky and stiff, and she always seemed to be half a beat behind the music. The worst moment came during a grand plié, when Amy rocked back and forth as she sank between her out-turned knees and almost went down on her bottom. This was going to be a bigger job than she'd thought, Elizabeth decided.

"Let me give you a pointer," she said. Amy looked embarrassed, but Elizabeth went on anyway. "I used to have trouble with pliés, too, but I figured out that if you keep your back perfectly straight, you can go down into the plié and up again without losing your balance."

Amy straightened her back and tried the plié again. This time she held her back straight and completed the move without wobbling at all.

"Gosh, thanks," she said. Her face was shining with gratitude. "Maybe you could help me with my pirouettes, too. I can't do them at all."

Elizabeth smiled. Pirouettes were one of her favorite steps. It would be fun teaching Amy to do them properly. "Sure, Amy. Just watch me and do what I do."

Elizabeth started with a demi-plié and then whirled around in a perfect pirouette. "Now you try it," she said.

Amy tried, but she held her arms wrong. She was off balance, and when she made the turn, she had to lunge forward to keep from falling. Patiently, Elizabeth showed her again, but once more Amy's pirouette was a disaster. Amy tried about a dozen more times, but it seemed to Elizabeth that she was getting worse.

Finally, it was four o'clock. "My mom must be here," Amy said. Elizabeth could see relief on her face.

"Try it one more time," she suggested.

Elizabeth held her breath as Amy whirled dizzily and crashed into the back of the sofa.

Amy grabbed her books and walked to the stairs. She put her sweater on over her tights and gathered up her clothes. "Thanks, Elizabeth. You really tried, but it's no use. Let's face it, I'll never be a dancer." She lowered her eyes dejectedly as she headed upstairs, leaving Elizabeth staring sadly after her.

Four

◇

Jessica left the Unicorn meeting the minute it was over. As soon as Janet Howell, the club's eighth-grade president, had called the meeting to order, Jessica remembered what it was that had been nagging at her all morning. She and Elizabeth were supposed to work with Amy Sutton on her ballet steps. Jessica knew she should have left the meeting that instant. But just then Lila Fowler had whispered, "Today I want to talk over some ideas for my Halloween party." Jessica knew that a party at Lila's was bound to be something special, so she decided to stay.

But even after an hour the party had not been mentioned at all. There had been the usual talk about clothes and boys, and then Mary Giaccio said that Ross Bradley, a tall eighth-grader, looked as if he were getting a mustache. The girls had giggled so hard about that, it had taken Janet a full ten minutes to get everyone quiet again. Finally, Jessica slipped Janet a note saying she had to leave because her mother wanted her to get home by four o'clock. Then she raced out, making the normally fifteen-minute trip from Lila's house in about half the time.

"Elizabeth?" she called as she burst in the door. "Elizabeth? Amy? I'm here. Are you practicing?"

Jessica listened for a moment. When no one answered, she went to the top of the basement stairs and called again, "Elizabeth. Where are you?"

"Right here," came a voice from behind her. "Amy just went home. Where have you been? You were supposed to be here to help her with her ballet steps."

For an instant Jessica felt a twinge of guilt at being so late, but then her eyes narrowed and she challenged her sister. "You know I had a special Unicorn meeting after school."

"Jessica, how was I supposed to remember?" cried Elizabeth. "After all, you did agree to practice with us today. Besides, you thought helping Amy was a great idea, and so would Madame André. She can't take time to help every single person in the class."

"Of course not. She's too busy watching you and telling the class how wonderful you are. How could she possibly have time for Amy Sutton or even for *me* with you around? Teacher's pet!"

"Jessica, I am not teacher's pet. I haven't done one thing to get Madame to like me. You're being unfair."

Elizabeth's face crumpled in despair, and she looked as if she might cry. For an instant Jessica regretted her words. She wasn't trying to hurt her sister. But slowly the memory of ballet class and Madame André complimenting Elizabeth over and over made her feel so bad, her chest filled with a dull ache. Elizabeth was teacher's pet all right, and her denying it wouldn't change a thing.

At ballet class the next afternoon Jessica felt even worse. Madame André seemed to be praising Elizabeth more than ever.

"Elizabeth, your grand pliés have never been

better. It is obvious that you have been practicing very hard."

What about me? Jessica wanted to cry. *I've been practicing, too.* But if Madame noticed any improvement in Jessica's dancing, she kept it to herself.

To make matters worse, Madame singled out Amy Sutton for praise just before the class was ending.

"Amy," she said brightly. "You, too, have been working hard. I'm very pleased with your pliés."

Amy smiled self-consciously. "Thank you, Madame André. Elizabeth has been helping me."

"But of course. Elizabeth is a dedicated dancer," said Madame, giving Elizabeth a radiant smile.

Jessica felt her throat tighten and her eyes fill with tears. She had dreamed that Madame would say those words to her. If only she hadn't gone to that Unicorn meeting! No, she thought quickly. It was all Elizabeth's fault. Elizabeth had betrayed her!

For the next few days the twins managed to avoid speaking to each other. If Elizabeth was watching television when Jessica entered the family room, Jessica would go upstairs and talk on the phone instead. If Jessica was fixing a snack in the kitchen, Elizabeth would get an ice cream bar out of the freezer in the garage and eat it outside under the old pine tree. Even at mealtimes they did not speak.

"Steven, will you ask Elizabeth to pass the mashed potatoes, please?" Jessica would say, smiling sweetly at her brother and then glaring at her sister behind his back.

Elizabeth, too, would smile at Steven as she handed the mashed potatoes to him. "Tell Jessica to eat my share," she would say innocently. "I'm watching my weight for the recital."

When Jessica was alone, she thought of nothing but the audition. Surely if she practiced and knew her steps perfectly, Madame André would have to choose her to be Swanilda, she thought over and over again.

The closer the day for the audition came, the harder Jessica practiced. Each time the tone arm dropped onto the practice record and the music began, Jessica forgot all about her sister and Madame André and getting the lead in the recital. She was transported to another world, where she danced among fluffy pink clouds and soared and dipped with the grace of a bird. And each time the music ended, she would smile and think how much she loved to dance.

The day of the audition finally arrived. There was the usual icy silence between the girls at the breakfast table. Mrs. Wakefield sighed. "It's only nine o'clock, and the audition isn't until three," she said. "Would anyone like to go to the mall with me this morning? They're having a big sale today."

Jessica loved to shop. She wanted to say yes, but this was her last chance to practice before the audition. "Count me out," she said reluctantly. "I have other plans."

"I'll go," Elizabeth volunteered. Getting away from Jessica seemed like a good idea.

Jessica watched her mother back the van out of the driveway and felt an immense sense of relief. Steven had gone to a friend's house, and her father was at his office going over some papers. That meant she had the whole house to herself and lots of time to practice.

Speeding toward her room to change into dancing clothes, she stopped short when the phone rang.

"Hello," she said.

"Elizabeth? You are on the line, *n'est-ce pas*?"

The strong French accent could mean only one person.

"No, Madame André, this is Jessica."

"Oh, no matter," she said. "I am calling to tell both of you that the time for the audition has been changed. Everyone is to be at the studio dressed and ready to dance promptly at eleven this morning. Do you have that, Jessica?"

"Yes, Madame. The audition has been changed to eleven this morning," said Jessica, trying to keep the excitement out of her voice. She smiled as she hung up the phone. Madame André didn't know it, but she had done Jessica a big favor.

Five

◇

Jessica tapped her fingertips on the telephone excitedly. What luck! The audition was just over an hour away. There was no way Elizabeth could make it.

There was no use leaving Elizabeth a note, she decided. It wouldn't do any good. She'd never be back from shopping in time. "Poor Elizabeth," Jessica murmured. "It looks like she'll miss the audition. I know she'll be crushed, especially since Madame André could never give the lead to anyone who didn't try out."

Jessica's heart was pounding with excitement as she hurried to her room. It was almost too wonderful. Her biggest competition wouldn't even show up. Still, she wanted to look her best, and she took out her new white leotard and matching tights, pulled her best white ballet slippers off their special shelf in the closet, and stuffed everything into the pink canvas bag that she used for dance class. Then she went to the mirror and fastened her golden hair up into a bun. "Perfect!" she said to herself. Satisfied, she smiled approvingly.

Downstairs Jessica glanced at the kitchen clock. She had just enough time to get to the corner to catch the bus. She started to walk toward the front door, but stopped, sighing deeply. She couldn't forget about Elizabeth. Maybe she should leave a note after all. Her twin would be terribly hurt if she weren't told of the change of time for the audition. She might even think that Jessica didn't want her there. Besides, Jessica reasoned, it might save her sister a trip to the Dance Studio after Madame André and everyone else had gone home.

Jessica took a piece of paper from the message pad beside the phone and scribbled a hasty note.

Dear Liz,
   I've looked for you everywhere. Madame André has changed the audition to eleven this morning.

                                    Love, Jess

She attached the note to the center of the refrigerator door with a magnet shaped like a chocolate-chip cookie. *There,* she thought smugly. *No one can say I didn't try.* Then she raced out the door to catch her bus.

The girls in Madame André's ballet class were scurrying around the dressing room in their practice clothes. Everyone was nervous about the audition except Jessica.

"I'm so scared, I'm going to *die!*" shrieked Kerry Glenn.

Jo Morris's eyes grew large with fright. "My legs have gone numb. I can't feel them anymore. Honest. How am I going to dance if I can't even feel my legs?"

Jessica looked around the room and felt better and better about her chances at getting the lead. She had to swallow a giggle when she noticed Amy Sutton sitting on a bench in one corner of the dressing room. Amy was trembling, and her teeth seemed to be chattering as if she were sitting at the North Pole instead of in Madame André's dance studio.

Amy's eyes had a glazed look, but they came sharply into focus when she spotted Jessica.

"Where's Elizabeth?" she asked, sounding genuinely alarmed. "She is coming, isn't she?"

Jessica shrugged. "Who knows? She ran off shopping with my mom."

Amy shot up from the bench like an erupting volcano. "You've got to find her, Jessica. She can't miss the audition."

By this time most of the others had heard the conversation. They were crowding around Jessica asking questions and offering suggestions.

"Do you know where she went?"

"Maybe she's at the mall."

"Could you call there and have her paged over the loudspeaker?"

"Girls! Come into the studio at once. It's time for the audition to begin." Madame André's voice was loud and commanding, and the dressing room grew silent immediately.

Jessica felt a tingle of anticipation travel up her spine as she followed the others into the studio and made a low bow to Madame. Again, the Coppelia doll sat in a chair, looking toward the class. Jessica scarcely noticed. Only one thing mattered now: the audition was about to begin.

Madame André returned the bow and then said, "Everyone to the barre, please. We will warm up first. Then when it is time to dance, I will call you forward one by one in alphabetical order."

Jessica saw Cammi Adams shiver as the girls took their places at the barre. Cammi was a good dancer, but Jessica could see that being the first one to audition was making her nervous.

The warm-up was over quickly, and Madame André motioned for the class to sit cross-legged on the floor. "Cammi Adams, center, please," Madame called sharply.

Cammi hurried to the middle of the floor and stood poised for only an instant before the music began. She danced stiffly at first, and her face wore the expression of concentration. As she neared the end of the piece, she began to relax. Jessica watched her closely all through her audition. Cammi was good. *But she's not as good as I am*, Jessica thought smugly.

Kerri Glenn was next. She shot a terrified look at Jessica as she took her place and waited for the music. Like Cammi, she was stiff at first and obviously nervous. She almost collapsed with relief when the music stopped and she returned to sit with the class. The next three girls were more relaxed, thought Jessica, but they were not really any competition. Jo Morris came next, and she was the best so far.

As the audition progressed, Jessica's confidence rose even more. There was still no sign of Elizabeth as Amy Sutton took her place to dance. The Wakefield twins were the only ones left after Amy. For once Jessica felt that being the last one called would be an advantage. There would be no doubt that she was the best dancer and deserved the starring role.

A gasp from the class startled Jessica. She looked up just in time to see Amy lose her balance trying to pirouette and come crashing to the floor. The girls stared silently for a moment, and then Amy scrambled to her feet and finished her dance. Her face was red as she went back to her place on the floor.

"Elizabeth Wakefield," Madame called out in her commanding voice.

"Elizabeth isn't here, Madame," said Jessica.

Madame André frowned, and Jessica could see that she was terribly displeased that Elizabeth was not there. "And just exactly where is she?" Madame demanded.

"I don't know," Jessica answered. "I guess she

just wasn't interested in coming." *Or anyway*, Jessica thought to herself, *if Elizabeth really cared about the auditions, she would have stayed home to practice instead of running off shopping.* Madame André was obviously very upset. "All right, Jessica," she said. "You may dance for me now."

As soon as the music began, Jessica forgot about Madame André and was lost in the beautiful dance. Jessica could feel herself swirling in perfect time to the music, graceful and beautiful, the perfect Swanilda. When the last strains died away, Jessica bowed and looked quickly at Madame André for a sign that she had liked what she had seen.

Madame's face was as blank as Coppelia's, and she glanced again toward the door. Finally, she sighed deeply and raised her hand for attention. "Thank all of you for dancing for me. I was pleased at how well each one of you performed. On Tuesday afternoon I will announce—"

Suddenly, the studio door burst open, and a breathless Elizabeth rushed in.

Six

◇

Elizabeth hesitated just long enough to bow to Madame André and then ran straight to Jessica, throwing her arms around her twin and hugging her tightly.

"Oh, Jessica. You're a wonderful sister. If you hadn't left that note for me, I would have missed the audition!"

Jessica felt as if an icy hand were squeezing her heart. "Gee, Elizabeth. It's great that you got home so early and found my note," she said, trying to sound pleased even though she felt like sinking through the floor.

"Mom forgot her credit cards. Can you believe that? We went back to get them, and I saw your note up on the fridge. Thanks to you, I'm here in time. I am in time, aren't I, Madame André?"

"Of course, Elizabeth. Of course! Now, run along and change into your dancing clothes. All of us want to see you dance."

Jessica sank to the floor, sitting beside the rest of the class. It was no use now. Elizabeth had gotten to the studio in the nick of time.

Jessica's hopes rose as she watched Elizabeth dance. She was good, but her jumps were not as high as Jessica's and her fouettés were slower. Maybe there was a chance for her after all, Jessica thought excitedly. Surely Madame had to see how much better she was than Elizabeth—even if Elizabeth was teacher's pet. Teacher's pet. The words made Jessica's spirits sink again. No one could compete with a teacher's pet, she thought hopelessly.

Madame André's face was glowing when the music stopped and Elizabeth finished her dance. Madame began applauding, first toward Elizabeth and then toward the whole class. "You are all wonderful," she cried. "Now, don't forget," she said, pausing and holding up a finger for emphasis, "Tuesday afternoon I shall announce the dancers for the parts of Swanilda and the four dolls, and we shall all begin working very hard to get ready for our recital. Class dismissed!"

When the twins got home, Elizabeth headed straight for her room and Jessica plopped down on the sofa in the den. She didn't even want to be in the same part of the house as her twin right now. Not after what had happened. How could her mother have forgotten her credit cards? She'd never done anything like that before. But today she had, and Elizabeth had gotten to the audition in time. Now Madame André would give her the solo part for sure.

"Hey, Jess. What do you think?"

The voice was definitely Steven's, but when Jessica looked up, a silver-wrapped figure stood beside the sofa.

Jessica gasped. "What on earth are you doing?"

"This is my robot costume for Halloween. I think I used up all of the aluminum foil in the supermarket. How do I look?"

"Fabulous. Now leave me alone. I have more important things to think about right now than Halloween," Jessica grumbled.

"What could be more important than Halloween? It's only a month away," Steven insisted, "and I've got some great plans."

Jessica threw her brother a look of disgust as she got up from the sofa and headed for her room. Halloween might be only a month away, but she wouldn't be able to think about anything until Madame André made her announcement on Tuesday. That was three days away, thought Jessica. Three *long* days that she would have to be right there in the same house with Elizabeth.

In her own room Elizabeth sighed and tingled with excitement. How could she wait until Tuesday afternoon to find out if she would get the solo part?

She pictured the audition again. Madame André had been so pleased to see her even though she had gotten there very late. She had danced well except for a few steps that gave her trouble. But then, she decided, she had only begun to study ballet. She knew she would get better with practice. After all, Madame was always complimenting her on how well she was progressing.

Elizabeth waltzed around the room, humming to herself and imagining how it would feel to dance a solo in front of an audience. "And if I get to do it," she whispered. "It will all be because of Jessica's note."

"Hey, Elizabeth." Steven's voice came through her door. "Phone!"

Elizabeth had been so absorbed in her day-dream that she hadn't heard the telephone ring.

"Coming," she called as she walked to the phone. She picked up the receiver and said hello.

"Hi, Elizabeth. This is Amy."

"Hi, Amy. What's up?"

"Not much. Mom picked me up right after the audition, so I didn't get a chance to talk to you then. Mostly I just called to say how glad I am that you made it on time. Madame André was really upset when you weren't there earlier."

"It was a good thing Jessica left me a note about the time change. Didn't she explain to Madame that I'd gone shopping with my mother?"

When Amy didn't answer, Elizabeth frowned and asked, "Well . . . didn't she?"

"Not exactly," said Amy.

"What do you mean, not exactly? What *exactly* did she say?"

"She said she didn't know where you were," said Amy. "And—"

"And what?"

"She said you weren't interested in coming to

the audition. I couldn't believe it. I mean, I know how much you like to dance."

Elizabeth could feel her heart thudding in her chest. So Jessica didn't want her at the audition. She'd told Madame André and everyone else that Elizabeth hadn't wanted to come!

"I have to go now, Amy," Elizabeth said into the receiver. "I'll talk to you later." She hung up the phone and raced blindly back to her room. Jessica's note still lay on her desk. She wadded it into a ball and hurled it into a corner. Then she sank down onto her bed.

Seven

That weekend was one of the longest Elizabeth had ever lived through. She avoided Jessica as much as she could, but she could not avoid the terrible knowledge that her twin had wanted her to miss the audition. Elizabeth wondered over and over again why Jessica would do something so awful. Jessica had just as much chance with Madame André as Elizabeth. She'd always had. What was wrong with her?

Elizabeth tried to write an article for *The Sweet Valley Sixers* about the Halloween festivities coming up at school. Usually, writing got her mind off her problems and made her feel better, but not this time. All she could think about was Jessica.

Jessica, too, spent a miserable weekend. She kept seeing the look on Madame André's face when Elizabeth arrived at the audition. "She might as well have announced Swanilda right then," Jessica muttered aloud. "Anyone could see that Elizabeth was the only one who had a chance."

Jessica thought about how confident the Unicorns were that she would star in the recital. "I'm sure that nobody else has a chance against you," Lila Fowler had said. "You're the only Unicorn in the class, and everybody knows that Unicorns are very pretty and *very* special." What would they say if she didn't get the lead? But how could she when her own twin sister was teacher's pet?

Everyone hurried to dance class after school on Tuesday, hoping that Madame André would make the announcement at once. The girls were so excited before class that scarcely anyone said a word as they changed into their leotards and tights. When they entered the studio, Madame André was arranging Coppelia in the chair by her desk. She did not turn to the class until all the girls had lined up to make their bows.

"Good afternoon, Madame André," they said at the same time, just as they always did.

"Good afternoon, class," she answered with a nod. "First position at the barre, *s'il vous plaît*."

The girls groaned in disappointment and lined up at the barre. Jessica's heart was pounding so loudly that she was sure Madame André could hear it. *Oh, please, please, let me get the part,* she thought as she went through the familiar routine. She glanced at Madame out of the corner of her eye, but the teacher wore the same expression as on any other day.

Elizabeth could scarcely hear the music over the beating of her heart. Would she get the solo part? She was still having trouble with some of her fouettés and jetés. No matter how hard she worked on them, she could not do them right. But if they were really bad, then surely Madame André had noticed, too.

Elizabeth thought about Jessica's dancing. Her sister never seemed to have trouble with fouettés and jetés, at least not when Elizabeth was looking. Of course, she wasn't looking every second. Jessica probably had problems with lots of steps, she reasoned. It was just that she'd never noticed.

The barre warm-up was finally over. "Center, please, everyone," Madame ordered. The girls were all waiting for the important announcement, but Madame said nothing about the recital. "Heads up. Shoulders low. Backs straight. Sloppy, sloppy, sloppy today! How will we ever be ready for the performance?"

The girls scurried to their places in the center of the studio, exchanging worried glances. It was obvious that Madame wasn't pleased. But how could she expect them to be at their best? Jessica wondered. If only she would tell them who would dance Swanilda!

Madame André paced back and forth in front of the class as they went through their steps. "Amy, tuck in your bottom," she said sternly. "And, Grace, where do your *arms* belong?"

Finally, the music stopped, and Madame André sighed deeply as she shook her head. "I want you all to go home and practice, practice, *practice!*" she commanded. "Class is dismissed. And, oh, yes," she said as her eyes widened. "The solo parts. I promised to announce this afternoon the names of the girls who have the solo parts." Madame walked over to her desk and picked up a sheet of paper. She looked at it very carefully, as if she had never seen it before. Finally, she looked up at the class and spoke. "The four dolls will be Cammi Adams, Jo Morris, Kerri Glenn, and Melissa McCormick." There was a ripple of applause as Madame flashed a smile at each of the four girls, who were giggling and hugging each other. There was only one more part to be announced, the most important one. Both Elizabeth and Jessica shot nervous glances at each other, knowing that the big moment had finally arrived. "The part of Swanilda," Madame said, and paused dramatically, "will be danced by Elizabeth Wakefield."

Elizabeth hugged herself with joy. It was too wonderful to be true. She had gotten the part after all . . . in spite of her sister. But what about Jessica? Elizabeth turned just in time to see her twin racing toward the dressing room. In a burst of anger Elizabeth caught up to her.

"Jessica Wakefield, I know that you never thought I'd get home early enough to see that note and get to the audition on time. You wrote it only to make yourself look good. Then you told everyone that I didn't care enough about the audition to show up. Well, I got the part anyway."

Jessica's face was white. "It wouldn't have mattered if you hadn't gotten to the audition on time,"

Jessica countered. "It wouldn't have mattered if you hadn't gotten there at all! You're teacher's pet! Madame loves you, and she hates me even though I'm a much better dancer than you are!"

Hot tears stung Elizabeth's eyes, but before she could answer, the rest of the class streamed into the dressing room.

Grace Oliver raced to Elizabeth, hugging her and shouting, "Oh, Elizabeth. Congratulations!"

Everyone began laughing and congratulating Elizabeth, talking at the same time, and hopping around excitedly.

"Aren't you scared to death?" cried Kerri, opening her eyes wide. "I am!"

"Not yet," Elizabeth conceded. "But I probably will be by the night of the recital."

Jessica drifted off by herself so that no one would see how sad she felt. It wasn't fair. Couldn't anybody see that? How could Madame André be so blind? How could she be so mean and spiteful?

As the excitement subsided, Elizabeth looked around for Jessica, but she was nowhere to be seen. *Jessica always wants to be the center of attention*, Elizabeth thought grimly as she began changing her clothes. *She's gone off somewhere to pout and think terrible things about me. Well, it won't do her any good.*

Nothing she can do can change things. I have the part of Swanilda, and that's all there is to it.

A few moments later Elizabeth caught sight of Jessica again. She had seemed to reappear out of nowhere, and she slowly began changing out of her dance clothes. Suddenly, Elizabeth was filled with pity. *Jessica wanted the solo part as much as I did,* she thought. *Maybe even more. I really shouldn't feel so angry toward her. She probably just wanted to be by herself for a few minutes while everyone was congratulating me.*

Suddenly, Madame André came rushing into the dressing room. "Something terrible has happened," she cried. Her face was creased with concern. "Coppelia is missing!"

Eight

◇

Jessica smiled to herself as the others rushed to help Madame search the studio for the missing doll. She did not join them. It served Madame André right to have her doll stolen, she thought. Maybe it would wreck the entire recital. She pictured Cammi and Kerri and Jo and Melissa, and especially Elizabeth, crying their eyes out. It would serve them all right.

She stuffed her leotard and tights into her canvas bag and slipped out of the studio while no one was looking. But instead of heading for home, she stopped and leaned against the building. For the hundredth time she saw the vision of herself performing Swanilda. She could hear the music as she did a perfect pirouette. She could hear the audience applauding wildly. But as her eyes cleared, she was once more standing beside the studio instead of onstage at Sweet Valley High School. Tears filled her eyes. Why had Madame André been so unfair?

Jessica wiped away her tears with the back of her hand and started to walk home alone. When she reached the Wakefields' neat split-level house, she hurried inside and ran up to her room. She didn't want anyone to know she was there. It had been hard enough facing the class after Elizabeth got the solo part, but how could she ever face her parents?

A few minutes later she heard Elizabeth come home. Opening her bedroom door a crack, Jessica listened as Elizabeth broke the news to their mother.

"Mom, guess what? I got the lead! I'm going to be Swanilda! Isn't that great?"

"Elizabeth, that's wonderful," Jessica heard her mother exclaim. "It's a shame that both you and Jessica couldn't dance the solo, but I'm sure your sister's happy for you, too."

Jessica closed the door as tears welled up again. How could anyone expect her to be happy for Elizabeth? It was totally unfair!

Downstairs, Mrs. Wakefield put her arm around Elizabeth. "I'm really proud of you. All your hard work paid off!"

"It *was* a lot of work," Elizabeth admitted. "But I'm glad I practiced. It's hard to believe, though, that I'm actually going to dance the solo. Ooooh! It makes me shiver just to think about it."

Elizabeth danced around the room with excitement. She closed her eyes and tried to imagine the scene, but instead of a stage she saw Jessica's face, teary-eyed and miserable, just the way she knew her twin must be right now.

"Mom, what about Jessica?" Elizabeth asked. "What am I going to do? She worked hard, too. I've never seen her try so hard. She keeps saying Madame André picked me because I'm her pet. But I never did anything to try to get Madame to like me. That can't be true. Can it?"

"Of course not, dear. Jessica is used to getting what she wants, and she wanted that solo part very much. It may take a little time, but I'm sure she'll be happy for you."

Elizabeth sighed. "I sure hope so."

Upstairs in her room, Jessica was anything but happy. The ache in her heart was almost too much to bear. "It isn't fair," she whispered over and over again to her image in the mirror. "I danced much better than Elizabeth. Why doesn't Madame André like me?"

A soft knock sounded at the door. *Elizabeth!* Jessica thought. *She can't just leave me alone. She has to come into my room and rub it in.*

"Go away," Jessica called. "I'm busy."

"Come on, Jess. Let me in a second."

It was Steven. What could he want? she wondered.

"OK, but only for a minute."

The door swung open and in came Steven, once again dressed for Halloween. This time he was covered with an old khaki army blanket with holes cut in it for his eyes. The blanket was almost covered with leaves and dead branches, which Steven had obviously glued to it.

"The Creature from the Black Lagoon at your service. How do I look?"

Jessica stared at him in amazement. "Disgusting," she said.

"Great! That's what I like to hear!"

"I thought you were going to be a robot."

"I changed my mind. The foil was too shiny. It would be impossible to sneak up on the Mercandy house wearing that stuff. But in *this* . . ."

Jessica didn't answer. Everyone in Sweet Valley said that the Mercandys' run-down mansion was haunted. Kids always went there on Halloween to play pranks on old Mr. and Mrs. Mercandy. Ordinarily, the mere mention of the Mercandy place sent shivers up and down Jessica's spine, but today she was too upset over losing the part of Swanilda to care.

"So what do you think?" Steven insisted. "Do I make a good Creature from the Black Lagoon or not?"

"You make a great one. Now go scare somebody else. I'm busy."

Steven shrugged and backed out the door, making disgusting sounds as he went. Tears welled up in Jessica's eyes again. She hadn't been very nice to her brother, but she couldn't help it. Why didn't anyone understand how miserable she felt?

Jessica was still brooding a few minutes later when another knock sounded at her bedroom door.

"What does he want now?" she grumbled. She started to yell at Steven to go away again, but changed her mind. She would just ignore him instead.

The knock came again, this time louder and more insistent. Angrily, Jessica went to the door and pulled it open. "What do you want now?" she demanded, and then she gasped. It wasn't Steven, but her mother.

"Gosh, Mom." She fumbled for words. "I thought it was Steven again."

Mrs. Wakefield smiled sympathetically. "So he's been showing you his Halloween costume, too, huh? May I come in?"

"Sure." Jessica shrugged.

Mrs. Wakefield sat down on the edge of the bed. Reaching out to clasp her daughter's hands, she began to speak gently. "Jessica, I know how hard it was for you to lose the solo part, and I want you to know that I understand that, and so does Elizabeth. But I don't understand why you keep saying that you lost it unfairly."

Jessica's heart leaped into her throat. "Mom, it's true! You should see how much better I dance than Elizabeth. The only reason Elizabeth got that part is that Madame André likes her better than me!"

"Jessica," Mrs. Wakefield said firmly. "I'm sure Madame André is a devoted teacher. She would never treat anyone unfairly. Besides, Elizabeth is your twin sister. You should be happy that the solo went to someone in the family."

"But, Mom," Jessica insisted, "you don't understand."

"I do understand, Jessica. And what's more, you're being a very poor sport. I hope that I won't have to talk to you about this again."

Jessica watched her mother leave the room. Then she burst into tears. "But Madame André *is* unfair," she sobbed into her pillow. "And *you're* unfair. And *Elizabeth's* unfair. And *everybody's* unfair!"

Nine

Elizabeth tossed and turned all night thinking about her sister. Jessica hadn't only lost the part of Swanilda, but she had not even been chosen for one of the other solos. Poor Jessica, Elizabeth thought. It was easy to understand why she was heartbroken.

Something else was bothering Elizabeth, too. She could not forget about Coppelia's mysterious disappearance or about the few moments in the dressing room when everyone was congratulating her. She had looked around the entire room, but Jessica was nowhere to be seen. A moment later

Madame André had announced that the doll was missing. And it was very strange that Jessica was the only one in the class who did not help Madame André search for the doll.

Jessica couldn't possibly have taken it, Elizabeth told herself for the hundredth time. Jessica wouldn't do a thing like that—not even to get back at Madame for giving the solo to Elizabeth. But who else would take a life-size doll? Who else had a reason?

Elizabeth got out of bed the next morning more determined than ever to find a way to make up with Jessica. It scared her to think that her sister might actually have taken the doll just because she didn't get the solo part. She couldn't let Jessica be so unhappy. But what could Elizabeth do? How could she stop the situation from getting any further out of control?

Jessica hadn't slept much that night. She had spent hours lying awake thinking about how to tell the Unicorns that Elizabeth would star in the recital. Then she made her decision. She had no choice but to tell them the truth.

The next morning the Unicorns were congregated on the front steps of the school. Jessica hurried over to them.

"Hi, Jessica," said Lila Fowler. "Did you find out about the solo part yet?"

"You did get it, didn't you?" asked Ellen Riteman.

"Of course not," Jessica answered matter-of-factly. "I *am* the best dancer, but I'm not teacher's pet."

"I hate teacher's pets," said Kimberly Haver. "They're always so goody-goody."

"So who's this teacher's pet who stole the solo part away from you?" Lila asked angrily.

"My own dear sister." Jessica loaded her voice with sarcasm. "Elizabeth got the lead part."

"Elizabeth? You're kidding," said Lila.

"I can believe it," said Kimberly. "Remember how she acted when she came to our Unicorn meeting? What a goody-goody!"

"You can say that again," said Mary Giaccio.

Jessica bit her lip to keep from saying anything. Her sister was a bit of a goody-goody, of course, but it bothered her to hear anyone else say it. After all, Elizabeth was her identical twin, and even though she did have her faults, no one had the right to criticize her.

"I'll bet you're really furious," said Ellen.

"Not really," Jessica replied, hoping to sound casual. "At least we kept it in the family."

Jessica felt pleased with herself when the first bell rang and she headed for class. She had told the Unicorns the truth. And even though she wouldn't be dancing the starring role, they all understood why she did not get it.

Elizabeth and Amy had just sat down in the cafeteria at lunchtime when Caroline Pearce stopped at their table. Although Caroline wrote a column for *The Sweet Valley Sixers*, Elizabeth had groaned softly when she saw her coming. Caroline was the biggest gossip in Sweet Valley Middle School.

"Have you heard what the Unicorns are saying about you, Elizabeth?" Caroline asked in a hushed voice. "It's all over school."

"What the Unicorns are saying about me? No. Why would they say anything about me?"

Caroline looked triumphant. "They're saying the only reason you got the lead in your dance recital is that you're teacher's pet. I wonder where they got an idea like that?"

A stab of anger replaced the sympathy Elizabeth had been feeling for Jessica all morning. She knew exactly where the Unicorns had gotten the idea. Only one person would call her teacher's pet.

"From Jessica, of course. She's a sore loser, and she can't admit that someone else could be better than she is at something." Elizabeth regretted her words the instant they were out. She should never have said something like that, especially in front of Caroline. Caroline would run straight back to Jessica and repeat every word. Soon the whole school would know.

So what? Elizabeth thought bitterly. It was Jessica who had started the rumors in the first place. And it was Jessica who had tried to keep her from auditioning for the solo part. It was probably even Jessica who took Coppelia! She wanted to ruin the recital and get even with Madame for giving someone else the lead. *That does it*, she thought. *This is war!*

Ten

◇

Elizabeth was determined not to do or say anything to Jessica, not after the terrible rumor she had started. At home that evening she paced back and forth outside the door to the basement for more than an hour. She was waiting for her turn to practice her solo. Jessica had been pretending ever since dinner that she had no idea Elizabeth needed to practice, too. Finally, Elizabeth couldn't stand it any longer. She opened the door and bounded down the basement stairs.

"Jessica, will you stop hogging the barre?" she commanded. "I have to practice, too, you know."

"Why do you have to practice? You've got it made. You know Madame André will tell you you're a wonderful dancer no matter how terrible you are."

"Terrible! How dare you call my dancing terrible!" cried Elizabeth. "You're just mad because you're not number one for once in your life and you can't stand it." Elizabeth burst into tears, stormed back up the stairs, and slammed the door behind her.

Jessica watched Elizabeth go, but she didn't feel sorry for her twin at all. She felt sorry for herself instead. She wasn't number one, at least not according to Madame André. And no matter how hard she practiced, she never would be. She was only wasting time practicing.

"Jessica, your father and I heard what you just said to your sister. It's time for another talk. Will you come up to the kitchen, please?"

Startled, Jessica looked up to see her mother standing in the doorway. It was clear from the tone of her voice that she meant business. Jessica squared her shoulders and went upstairs. She sat down at the kitchen table with her parents. Both her mother and father looked as solemn as jurors. Jessica swallowed hard. She knew what was coming.

"Your mother and I are very disturbed at the way you've been behaving over this recital," her father began.

"Why are you being so stubborn?" Mrs. Wakefield insisted. "Madame André has the right to choose anyone she wants to dance the lead. There's nothing you can do about that. You simply must accept it."

Jessica couldn't answer. Her heart felt as if it would burst. Elizabeth really was teacher's pet. Why wouldn't anyone believe her?

In her room Elizabeth stared out the window, wishing that the ballet recital were over. "I hate this whole thing," she said out loud. "What fun is it to be the star when Jessica and I do nothing but fight?"

She changed out of her leotard and tights. She didn't feel like practicing anymore, and thought about her predicament. She wondered over and over again what she was going to do. After a while she went looking for her mother and found her in her study working on some drawings.

"Mom," she began. "What am I going to do about Jessica? She practically hates me because I got the lead and she didn't. And she's telling everyone at school that the only reason I got it is because I'm teacher's pet."

Mrs. Wakefield looked sympathetically at her daughter. "I know, sweetheart. Your father and I heard what you said to her a little while ago. We talked to her, but I'm not sure it did any good."

"What am I going to do?" Elizabeth asked again. "Jessica had the same chance I had. She auditioned for Madame André, too, and Madame picked me. How can I prove to her that I'm not teacher's pet?"

"I don't think that you can," said Mrs. Wakefield. "I know how much you love your sister, and so do your dad and I, but we can't always give in to her just because she can't get what she wants every single time. It would be wrong, and it would be bad for Jessica."

"Thanks, Mom." Elizabeth sighed deeply. Her mother's advice was not what she had hoped it would be. She needed to know how to make things better. What her mother had said was that if she tried to make up with Jessica, things would get worse. But how could they? It seemed to Elizabeth that right now things were just about as bad as they could get.

*　　*　　*

With the recital getting closer, Madame André called another special practice on Saturday morning. The twins didn't say a word to each other as they walked to the Dance Studio the next morning. They turned their backs to each other as they changed into their dance clothes in the dressing room.

When the class filed into the studio a few minutes later, Madame looked very grim. She brought up the subject of the missing doll immediately.

"My poor Coppelia! As everybody knows, someone has taken our precious doll. I cannot imagine where she could be. Who would take her? But I'm afraid that is only part of the problem. I have tried and tried to find another life-size doll. I have called toy stores, department stores, doll hospitals—anyone who has anything to do with dolls. No one can tell me where to find another doll of that size. We must have a life-size doll! I ask you, do any of you have a doll the size of Coppelia that we can use in the recital?"

The hopeful look in Madame André's eyes faded as the girls looked questioningly at one another and all shook their heads. Elizabeth shot a quick glance at Jessica, but her twin's expression did not give her any clues to whether Jessica had stolen Coppelia.

"Well, then that is enough chatter for today," Madame announced abruptly. "*Corps de ballet*, center, *s'il vous plaît*. Swanilda, warm up at the barre while the corps is rehearsing."

Dutifully, Elizabeth went to the barre and began going through the routine. But out of the corner of her eye she could see the others practicing the chorus number. Most of all, she could see Jessica. Elizabeth caught her breath as her twin whirled around the room in perfect time to the music. She was a beautiful dancer, far better than anyone else in the corps.

She really is too good to be just one of the chorus, Elizabeth realized. The idea was disturbing, especially with all the trouble between them. *If only I had been here when she auditioned for Madame André,* thought Elizabeth. *Then I would know who the best dancer really is.*

"Elizabeth! You are supposed to be working, not daydreaming," Madame André called out. Elizabeth jumped. She hadn't realized that she had stopped when her thoughts turned to her sister. "And Elizabeth," Madame went on in a more kindly tone, "while I have your attention, let me work with you a bit. You are having a little trouble with a few of your steps."

Elizabeth felt relieved. Now surely she could overcome the problems she was having with the solo.

Madame André patiently instructed her on the proper way to execute the steps. Elizabeth tried over and over, but still she was having trouble.

"You are just nervous about the recital," Madame assured her. "Practice what I have shown you at home. I am sure you will master the steps soon."

Before she dismissed the class, Madame André gave each girl her costume for the recital. Elizabeth was scarcely aware of the ohs and ahs all around her as the others were handed their brightly colored dresses. All she could see was the beautiful blue costume of Swanilda, with yards and yards of netting underneath the skirt and shiny sequins covering the top. *I will practice at home*, she promised herself as she took the dress from Madame André. *I will be the best Swanilda ever!*

Jessica knew that Elizabeth hurried home from school every afternoon to work on her solo. She also knew that Elizabeth was trying very hard to get the steps just right in time for the recital. And every day Jessica noticed how much more nervous her twin was getting, so much so that her fouettés and jetés were getting worse instead of better.

On Friday afternoon, the day before dress rehearsal and just two days before the recital, Jessica sauntered down to the basement pretending to ignore Elizabeth, who was practicing her solo. Jessica opened the clothes dryer, hoping to find her new hot-pink sweatshirt there. She'd looked everywhere else, and the dryer was her final hope. She dug through the warm load of clothing, but didn't really notice what was there. Instead, she kept glancing at Elizabeth, who was working on the most difficult part of the solo, a series of pirouettes. Elizabeth always began correctly, in fourth position, but midway through the second turn she would wobble and lose her balance.

Jessica's anger and resentment began to melt as she watched Elizabeth try to master the turns, a look of utter panic on her face.

She's going to make a terrible Swanilda if she doesn't get that step right, thought Jessica. *She'll embarrass herself and Mom and Dad and me.* Jessica tried to fight down the tide of sympathy that was sweeping over her. Part of her wanted to see Elizabeth fail so she could say I told you so. But the rest of her couldn't forget that no matter what, Elizabeth was still the most important person in the world to her.

Finally, Jessica couldn't just stand there and do nothing. "Watch me, Elizabeth," she called out. "You aren't holding your head right. Keep it to the front as long as possible and then turn it really fast like this." Jessica assumed fourth position, moved into a pirouette, and continued to whirl around and around on one foot in a series of perfect fouettés.

Elizabeth caught her breath as Jessica moved across the floor. Her twin had never had a problem with fouettés. She could do them perfectly from the beginning.

Elizabeth tried again, holding her head the way Jessica had instructed. This time Elizabeth could feel the acceleration as she whipped her head around at just the right instant. She completed the step more gracefully than ever before.

"Wow," she said, a smile lighting her face. "That was a lot better, wasn't it?"

Jessica regarded her with cool eyes. "You need to work on your jetés, too. Watch this."

It was the same with Jessica's jetés. Her jumps were higher than anyone else's in the class. And as

Jessica explained the step, Elizabeth understood why. Again Elizabeth tried the jump, and again she could feel the improvement.

Then why was I chosen to dance the lead instead of Jessica? Elizabeth wondered. A cold feeling of dread settled over her. The question had been nagging at her for days, but she couldn't ignore it any longer. Was Jessica right? Was she really teacher's pet? She couldn't stand to be involved in something that unfair, especially if it meant Jessica was being hurt.

"Thanks, Jess," she said a few minutes later. "I think I can do them now." Elizabeth wanted to say more, but she knew that words alone would never help Jessica feel better.

That night Elizabeth tossed and turned, unable to fall asleep. Pictures flooded her mind of all the times Madame André had singled her out for praise, complimenting her and using her as an example for the rest of the class. And yet, she thought with amazement, Jessica was the best dancer all along. Why hadn't Madame André noticed her?

Elizabeth frowned and stared at the dark ceiling for a long time as the awful truth began to sink in. Jessica had been right all the time. Elizabeth *was* teacher's pet. That's why she had been chosen to dance the solo.

Tears trickled onto Elizabeth's pillow as she remembered how much fun it had been to get all the attention and flattery. *But poor Jessica,* she thought, *it should have been her. She loves dancing just as much as I love writing. What if Mr. Bowman had wanted Jessica to be editor of* The Sweet Valley Sixers *instead of me!* It would have been wrong, and Madame André was wrong.

Something had to be done. But what?

Eleven

◇

At dress rehearsal the next morning Elizabeth was still miserable. And Jessica's kindness was short-lived. She had been as cool as ever at the breakfast table, and ignored Elizabeth whenever she tried to talk to her. Obviously, she was sorry that she had helped Elizabeth the day before.

To make matters worse, Madame André had praised Elizabeth highly when she danced her solo for the class and got the steps almost perfect. "Now, see!" she had cried. "All it takes is practice."

Elizabeth leaned against the barre. She scarcely cared if she wrinkled her costume as she watched the corps go through its dance for a second time. She couldn't help but notice Jessica. Poor Jessica, she thought. Dressed in the same costume as the rest of the corps, she drooped like a wilted flower among the bright bouquet of dancers. She wasn't used to being one of the crowd.

Even though she was obviously miserable, Jessica danced beautifully, performing every step perfectly. *Why doesn't Madame André see how good she is,* Elizabeth wondered.

Finally, rehearsal was over and Madame motioned for the girls to sit around her on the floor. "I am desperate," she said, wringing her hands and looking at them with pleading eyes. "I *still* cannot find a doll for our recital. I have brought this one," she said, pulling a much smaller doll out of a paper bag. "But you can see, she will never do. She is much too small! Think again. Does anyone have a suggestion? We must have a Coppelia or our dance will be ruined."

When all the girls shook their heads sadly, Amy Sutton shyly raised her hand.

"Madame, I'll take her place," she offered. "I can sit on the stage and be very still. I know I can do it."

Madame stared at Amy in amazement. When

she finally spoke, her voice was soft. "You are very generous, Amy. Are you sure that you want to give up your chance to dance in the corps de ballet?"

"Oh, yes, Madame." Amy blushed. "I think I'd make a better Coppelia."

"It's settled then. And remember, everyone. Tomorrow is the big day! Practice! Practice! Practice!"

Elizabeth lingered in the dressing room while Madame gave Amy a costume and a dark wig for her role as Coppelia. She rushed up to her friend when she finally came back to change.

"I just want to tell you how nice I think you are for giving up your part in the recital to be Coppelia. What gave you such a super idea?"

Amy shrugged, looking embarrassed. "It's not giving up much when you dance the way I do," she said.

Elizabeth wondered if she was happier to be playing the role of the doll than dancing. She reached out and squeezed Amy's hand. "It's still a great idea," she told her.

Elizabeth went home after practice and rushed to the one place she could always go to be alone to think. It was an old pine tree in the backyard. The twins had played among its giant roots when they were younger, pretending it was a secret hideout. As they grew, the two of them went there when being twins was more important than being with other people. They knew they could sit there without anyone seeing them and talk over private things. But over the past year or so, Jessica had gotten tired of the old pine tree, and it had become Elizabeth's special place to dream or write or think over her problems. Like now.

She couldn't stop thinking about Amy Sutton. Amy would be so much happier and better being Coppelia than dancing in the corps. *If only I could switch roles with Jessica*, Elizabeth thought. *Then she could be the star, as she deserves.*

At first Elizabeth thought that maybe she should go to Jessica and offer to trade places. She would simply say, "Jessica, I think you should dance the part of Swanilda, and I'll take your place in the corps de ballet. You really deserve the lead, and you'll do a much better job than I ever could."

But Elizabeth knew that Jessica would never dance the solo if she got it that way. No, there had to be something else she could do, something that would convince Jessica that she *had* to dance the part of Swanilda.

Elizabeth sat among the pine roots until the

sun was low in the afternoon sky, but she could not come up with a plan. Even going to Madame André wouldn't work. Madame had made up her mind that Elizabeth should dance the lead, and nothing would change her mind. Elizabeth got up to head back to the house. It was getting late, and her parents might be wondering where she was.

Suddenly, she jolted forward, tripping over one of the roots and barely catching herself before she fell down on the grass.

For a ballerina, I'm not very graceful, she thought with an embarrassed laugh. But an instant later her laughter turned to joy. She had it! She had a plan.

Elizabeth thought about her wonderful idea all through dinner. She hardly noticed Jessica's angry glances in her direction. But it didn't matter what Jessica thought, because tomorrow everything would be OK again.

Right after dinner Elizabeth rushed to the phone and looked around quickly to make sure that Jessica wasn't nearby. Then she dialed Amy's number. Next to Jessica, Amy was her best friend, and Elizabeth had to tell someone about her great idea.

"Hi, Elizabeth," Amy said a minute later. "Getting nervous about tomorrow?"

"Yes, but it's not what you think. I know now

that Madame André made a mistake. Jessica should dance the solo part, not me."

"Elizabeth," Amy scolded her. "Don't tell me that Jessica has convinced you that you're teacher's pet."

"No," Elizabeth answered confidently. "I figured it out for myself when Jessica showed me how to do the steps I was having trouble with. She could do the steps perfectly all along. I should have seen it before. But worse, Madame André should have seen it. She was unfair, and I have to do something about it."

"But what?" asked Amy.

"Well, I've got a plan." Excitement filled Elizabeth's voice. "Tomorrow the whole family will load into the van to go to the recital. Everything will be fine until we get to the parking lot. Then, just as I get out, I'll pretend to step down wrong and twist my ankle. I'll pretend that it's really hurting and that there is no way that I can go onstage and dance. Jessica will have to take over."

"But Elizabeth, you'll miss the whole recital. You won't even get to be onstage. Besides, what if Jessica says no?"

"She won't say no," Elizabeth said confidently. "She's wanted to dance that solo for too long."

"But what about Madame André? What will she say about Jessica taking your part?"

"We're identical twins, silly. She won't know. At least not until the recital is over. Then she'll see what a wonderful dancer Jessica really is. Don't you see? It's a perfect plan."

"Gosh, Elizabeth. If you really think Jessica deserves the part, I suppose it's the right thing to do. But I still wish that you could dance the lead."

"Thanks, Amy."

The girls said good night and hung up. Elizabeth hurried to her room thinking that tomorrow would be a fantastic day after all.

Jessica was sprawled across her bed feeling as if it were the end of the world. Tomorrow was recital day, the day she had dreamed of for so long. Only now it was going to be a nightmare.

She rolled over onto her side and glared at the bright red peasant costume hanging on the knob of her closet door.

"It's ugly, and I hate it! And I look just like everybody else when I wear it!" she cried aloud. She picked up her pillow and threw it at the costume, sending it tumbling to the floor.

Elizabeth had been so cheerful all evening that

Jessica had wanted to throw up. She had stomped off to her room to be miserable alone. But now she had an idea. She got out of bed and walked to her dresser, smiling at the face in the mirror as if it were another person.

"I'll show them all," she said confidently. "I'll show Madame André, and I'll show Elizabeth, too! I won't wear that ugly costume. I won't dance in the corps de ballet. I won't even *go* to their stupid recital!"

Twelve

Elizabeth was awake long before her alarm went off the next morning. She had thought so much about faking a sprained ankle that she could almost feel it throbbing. It was a wonderful plan, and she knew it would work.

She dressed quickly, stopping only once to look wistfully at the beautiful costume of Swanilda. It made her sad to think that after all the long hours of practice she wouldn't get to wear the costume or even be in the recital. But it would be worth it, she thought resolutely.

Everyone was at the breakfast table except Jessica. In a way Elizabeth was relieved. It was going to be hard to keep her secret until it was time to leave for the recital.

"Well, if it isn't our star dancer," said Mr. Wakefield. "Are you all set for your big day?"

"'Morning, Dad," Elizabeth said, pouring cereal into a bowl. "I'm as set as I'll ever be, I guess. I'm already getting nervous."

"Break a leg!" declared Steven. Then he grinned sheepishly and added, "That's what they always say in show business, isn't it?"

Elizabeth nodded, fighting a giggle. Steven was closer to the truth than he realized. "Where's Jessica?" she asked.

At the sound of her name Jessica walked into the kitchen. As she sat down at the table, she looked more miserable than Elizabeth had ever seen her.

"I have an announcement to make," she said. "I am not going to the recital this afternoon."

"What!" Elizabeth cried. "You can't mean that. You have to go. You're part of the corps de ballet."

"The corps de ballet!" Jessica echoed bitterly. "That's just a fancy way of saying the chorus. No one will miss me if I'm not there."

"But Jessica," her mother insisted. "What about Madame André? She's counting on you."

"Madame André never noticed me before, so why would she notice today?" Angry tears filled Jessica's eyes.

"Honey, you shouldn't get so upset. There will be other recitals," said Mr. Wakefield.

"Fine," said Jessica. "I'll go to those, but I won't go to this one!"

Elizabeth fought to keep from panicking. This wasn't the way things were supposed to go. What was she going to do if Jessica refused to go to the recital?

"Boy, talk about being jealous," Steven said, shaking his head.

"Jealous!" shrieked Jessica. "How dare you call me jealous! It's true, Elizabeth is teacher's pet, and that's the only reason she's getting to dance the lead."

"You're staying home just because you can't stand to hear Elizabeth get all the applause," Steven bullied her.

Jessica gasped and stared wide-eyed at Steven for a moment. "Of course I can stand to hear Elizabeth get applause," she said, and Elizabeth was sure she heard a slight catch in Jessica's voice. "OK, I'll go to that dumb recital, but I won't dance. There! Are you satisfied?"

Jessica did not stay around for his answer. Instead, she jumped up from the table and stormed out of the room.

Elizabeth felt limp with exhaustion. She gave Steven a grateful smile. Then she headed for her own room. She planned to stay out of Jessica's sight until it was time to leave. She couldn't take a chance on anything else messing up her plan.

Jessica was sullen as she climbed into the van a few hours later. Her mother had insisted that she bring along her costume even though she wasn't planning to wear it because Madame André wanted all costumes returned to her right after the performance. Jessica tossed the peasant outfit into the empty seat beside her and stared at it as if it were a poisonous snake. She felt tears welling in her eyes as Elizabeth got in. She was carrying her beautiful blue costume.

Jessica was silent all through the short ride across town to the auditorium. She wished she hadn't let Steven trick her into coming. She knew she was going to be just miserable.

When they reached the parking lot, Jessica thought that maybe she could slip out of the crowded auditorium just before the recital started. She could say she was going to the ladies room, but she would really go outside and hide in the van. Later she could say that the ushers wouldn't let her back in after the recital started. She was picturing the whole scene and feeling a little better, when she heard a yelp of pain. Looking down quickly, she saw Elizabeth sitting on the pavement clutching her left ankle.

"What happened?" Jessica cried. "Lizzie, are you OK?"

Elizabeth looked up at her through tear-filled eyes. "Oh, Jess, I twisted my ankle. I jumped out of the van the way I always do. I don't know what happened."

Jessica was at her twin's side at once, and she and her mother formed a crutch to help Elizabeth to her feet.

"Can you step down on it?" Mrs. Wakefield asked.

"I don't know. I'll try. *Ouch!*" She tightened her grip on Jessica's shoulder and started to cry. "Oh, Jess. What am I going to do? I'll never be able to dance now."

Jessica looked at her sister in surprise. An idea flashed in her mind, but she dismissed it instantly. As badly as she wanted to dance the solo, she would never want to do it at her twin's expense.

"Let me have a look at that ankle," said Mr. Wakefield. Bending down, he pressed it gently, and then rotated it one turn in each direction. "It seems all right," he said. "Nothing's broken, anyway. I do think you ought to stay off it though. I'm sorry, sweetheart. I know how important the solo was to you."

"Oh, Jessica, you simply have to go on in my place," implored Elizabeth. "Without Swanilda the recital would be ruined."

Jessica hesitated. "But Lizzie, are you sure you can't dance? Madame André would be furious if anyone danced Swanilda but you."

Elizabeth put weight on her left foot and jerked up off the ground again. "Ouch! I can't, Jess. It's no use. You'll have to go on for me."

"But what about Madame André?" Jessica insisted.

"Don't tell her," Elizabeth said brightly. "If you're right and she chose me only because I'm her pet, she'll never know the difference."

Jessica's face lit up. "Oh, Lizzie. I'll do it! I'll be the best Swanilda in the world. You'll see!"

She grabbed the beautiful blue costume out of the van and raced toward the auditorium to change.

Thirteen

◇

The ushers were just beginning to seat people when Elizabeth, her parents, and Steven entered the building. The lobby of Sweet Valley High School was filled with nervous parents and grandparents, all eagerly awaiting the performance. Kids from school and people from town were starting to file in, too, and Elizabeth was filled with a mixture of happiness and sadness as she prepared to sit in the audience.

Jessica would make a wonderful Swanilda, she reminded herself as she tried to imagine the chaos in the dressing room. She hoped that in the excitement no one would recognize Jessica and spoil the plan.

"Elizabeth . . ."

Elizabeth turned at the sound of her name. To her surprise Amy Sutton stood beside her, wearing the peasant costume of the corps de ballet. In her hand was the dress and dark wig of Coppelia, which she handed to Elizabeth before she could speak.

"Amy, what is this? What are you doing?" asked Elizabeth, staring first at Amy, then at Coppelia's costume, and then back at Amy again.

"I want you to wear this," Amy said shyly. "You should at least be on stage, even if you don't get to dance."

Elizabeth started to protest. She knew that Amy would rather play Coppelia than dance and risk making a mistake. But Amy was looking at her with clear, confident eyes, and Elizabeth understood that it was her way of being a true friend.

"Thanks, Amy. You're super!" said Elizabeth.

She whispered the change of plans to her parents, and then together she and Amy headed backstage. Madame André was in conference with the piano player and far too busy to notice Elizabeth duck into the dressing room and slip on Coppelia's costume. Most of the other dancers, including Jessica, were already dressed.

Elizabeth could see her twin standing backstage, looking calm and beautiful. She was the perfect Swanilda, thought Elizabeth.

The recital was ready to begin. The modern dance class rushed past Elizabeth to find their places on the stage. A moment later the music swelled and they began their performance, but Elizabeth scarcely noticed. Her mind was on the trick that she and Jessica were playing on Madame. What if it didn't work? What if Madame realized that it was Jessica in Swanilda's costume and refused to let her go on? What would happen then? The recital would be ruined, not just for Madame, but for all of the girls in the class. And it would be all Elizabeth's fault.

Applause filled the auditorium as the first group of dancers finished their number. Only one more class would dance, and then Coppelia would be performed as the final number of the afternoon.

Again the audience responded with warm applause as the second-year class rushed back into the wings, breathless and glowing from a successful performance. It was time, and the corps de ballet lined up to go onstage.

Coppelia was to hold a book and sit in an alcove of the house where Coppelius, the dollmaker, had his workshop. Elizabeth sat down in the alcove while the girls dancing the parts of the other dolls took their places around the room. Her book was lying on the seat beside her. Elizabeth picked it up and wished a silent "good luck" to Jessica, Amy, and all her friends in the ballet class. Taking a deep breath, she prepared to watch the performance.

"Places, everyone," she heard Madame André call. Elizabeth struck the stiff pose of a doll. An instant later the music started, the curtain rose, and she caught her breath as the dance began. The first to come onstage were the corps de ballet, moving together in perfect step. Elizabeth wanted to smile even though she had to keep her face perfectly still. They had never danced so well in practice. Even Amy Sutton was graceful. Next were the solos of the dolls, and they, too, performed better than ever before.

Suddenly, the music changed. Elizabeth felt a tingling sensation travel up her back. She knew that music well. It was Swanilda's solo.

A hush fell over the audience as Jessica came onto the stage. She moved with extraordinary style and grace. Elizabeth forgot about being Coppelia as she watched her sister dance. Her eyes followed Swanilda's every move. Jessica truly did deserve the lead, Elizabeth thought.

Thunderous applause drowned out the last notes of the music as Jessica finished her solo and bowed low to the audience. She rose, smiling, to shouts of "Bravo! Bravo!"

As the audience began to file slowly out of the auditorium, Madame André hurried up the aisle. "Mr. and Mrs. Wakefield!" she called. "Please wait a moment." She began to pump Mr. Wakefield's hand the instant she reached them. "Congratulations. I must tell you, she is fabulous! A unique talent! My star pupil and she's never been better. I assure you that Elizabeth is the best Swanilda we have ever had!"

"I think you made a mistake, Madame André," Mrs. Wakefield said quietly. "That was not Elizabeth."

Madame André's eyes grew wide. "What! Not Elizabeth? What on earth do you mean?"

"Elizabeth hurt her ankle outside in the parking lot, and Jessica took her place. There wasn't time to explain to you then. It was too close to the performance."

"Surely it can't be," said Madame André. She

was shaking her head in disbelief. "Jessica could never dance that well. Oh, my . . ." Her words trailed off and her face clouded with sadness. "It is obvious that she can. How could I have been so blind? Excuse me, but I must find her and tell her how wonderful she was."

Jessica was standing alone in the middle of the stage thinking of her moment as a star, when Madame André came up behind her.

"Jessica! Jessica! You were fantastic!" Madame cried.

Jessica was stunned. So Madame had found out. "You aren't angry that I took Elizabeth's place?" she asked warily.

"I know all about that. It is a blessing that you knew the dance and could give such a wonderful performance."

Out of the corner of her eye Jessica could see someone rushing toward her wearing the costume of Coppelia. It was Amy Sutton. *No!* It was Elizabeth, and she wasn't even limping the slightest bit.

"Congratulations, Jessica. You were wonderful," cried Elizabeth.

"But what about your ankle?" asked Jessica. "I thought it was sprained. I thought you couldn't walk on it."

Elizabeth pulled off the dark wig of Coppelia and took a deep breath. "You were right, Jessica. You did deserve to dance the solo. I knew that when you helped me at home. I could see that you did all the steps perfectly all along. I was the one who was having trouble. It wasn't fair for me to dance Swanilda and let you dance in the corps. That was when I decided to trick you into changing places with me."

"Wow!" said Jessica. "It was a good thing I decided to come to the recital!" Jessica paused an instant. "Oh, Lizzie, thank you for all you did. You are the most wonderful sister in the world!"

Elizabeth turned to Madame André. "I hope you aren't angry with me. I guess I tricked you, too."

Madame André smiled and tears shone in her eyes. She put an arm around each twin and hugged them both. Then she said, "I am not angry. I am sorry that I made such a terrible mistake. I thought that Jessica was not serious at all about her ballet, but now I see how wrong I was. I hope you will forgive me. You are both stars!"

Amy Sutton had been standing nearby, and she heard Madame André's confession. With a deep sigh she approached the dance teacher.

"Madame André," she said, "I'm afraid that you're not the only one who needs to confess something." She looked down. "I'm the one who took Coppelia."

"What?" said Madame André. "Surely not you, Amy. Why on earth would you do a thing like that?"

"I was afraid of being in the recital. I'm a terrible dancer, and I was worried that I'd fall down and embarrass everyone. So I watched for a chance to take her when you were busy with something else. Then I hid her under a stack of props in the storage room, hoping that you wouldn't find her. I planned to volunteer to take her place all along."

"Oh, my precious Amy," said Madame André. "I'm so sorry that ballet is so hard for you. I am sorry you had to hide Coppelia. But I'm proud that you were such a good friend to Elizabeth. It was brave of you to put aside your fear so that she could be onstage with her sister. I am not angry with you. After all, not everyone is like Jessica—born to dance. Now, come along everyone. Let's go to my studio for a party. We have much to celebrate. A beautiful recital, wonderful friendships, and a brand new star!"

Fourteen

"Halloween is not too far off, and I've got a great idea for our costumes," Jessica said a few days later as the twins were bicycling home from ballet class. "Let's ask Madame André if we can borrow the recital costumes. Then I can be Swanilda one more time, and you can be Coppelia. Don't you think that's a great idea?"

Elizabeth frowned. "I'm not sure. What if something happens to the costumes while we're wearing them? Madame André would never forgive us."

"Oh, Elizabeth, don't be such a worrywart. What could possibly happen to them?"

"Have you forgotten last year already?" asked Elizabeth. "Our costumes were ruined!"

Jessica sighed. How could she forget? A whole gang of boys, including their own brother, Steven, had been playing their annual Halloween prank on old Mr. and Mrs. Mercandy. This time they were decorating their porch with shaving cream. When Mrs. Mercandy opened the door and screeched at them, they all ran off, only to find Jessica, Elizabeth, and some of their friends heading for a party on the next block. The shaving cream ended up all over the girls.

"That won't happen again," Jessica insisted. "Remember how Steven was grounded for two weeks after Dad found out what he did? Besides, I'm sure they'll think of something new and even meaner to do to the Mercandy place this year, so our costumes will be safe."

"I still don't think that asking Madame for the ballet costumes is a good idea," said Elizabeth.

"Well then, let's let Madame decide if it's a good idea," suggested Jessica. "Everybody in Sweet Valley knows that the Mercandy place is haunted and that Mrs. Mercandy is a witch and keeps crazy old Mr. Mercandy locked in the attic. I'm sure Madame André heard all about what goes on Halloween night. If she's worried that something will happen to the costumes, she'll just say no. Oh, come on, Lizzie. Let's ask her."

"Honestly, Jess. Just thinking about the Mercandy place and Halloween gives me the creeps," said Elizabeth.

Jessica let out a squeal of joy. "Me, too! Hey, let's ride our bikes by there on our way home! It will help us get into the mood for Halloween."

Before Elizabeth could say anything, Jessica had rounded a corner heading toward the street where the old Mercandy house stood.

"Jessica! Come back!" Elizabeth shouted. But her twin ignored her. Elizabeth did not wish to argue, so she pedaled after Jessica. She didn't like to go past the ugly old house, but she couldn't let Jessica go alone.

As the twins neared the Mercandy mansion, they were careful to stay on the opposite side of the street. Jessica had heard that anyone who got close to the house would be snatched inside and never heard from again. She didn't want to find out if the story was true.

When they were almost across from the house, they stopped their bikes and peered out at it from behind a tree.

"I thought you were scared of the Mercandy house," Elizabeth whispered.

"I'm just in a spooky mood," Jessica said. "But believe me, I'm not getting any closer. Don't those windows upstairs look creepy? They look like devil's eyes, and they're staring straight at us."

"Jess, stop that!" Elizabeth insisted. "The old place is scary enough. Let's get out of here."

Just as they started to leave their hiding place, a taxi moved slowly up the street and stopped in front of the Mercandy mansion.

"Don't tell me they have company," Jessica said with a gasp. "Who on earth would visit the Mercandys?"

The twins watched in fascination as a dark-haired girl about their own age got out of the taxi. She walked right up to the house and set a small cardboard suitcase on the porch. The taxi driver looked around nervously before pulling a larger suitcase out of the trunk and starting after her. Suddenly, he stopped. He looked as if something had made him change his mind about carrying the suitcase any farther, and he set it on the curb.

"This is as far as I go, miss," the twins heard him say.

The girl pushed a lock of long dark hair out of her eyes and looked sadly first toward the house and then toward the driver. "That's OK." She walked back to the curb and handed him some money. The driver looked relieved as he hurried back to his cab and drove away, leaving the girl alone in front of the house.

Elizabeth tapped Jessica on the shoulder and whispered as softly as she could, "Maybe we should say something to her. You know, ask her if she's certain she's got the right house."

Jessica's eyes widened as she looked back at her sister. "You've got to be kidding."

"Oh, come on, Jess. It scares me to think of her actually going into that house."

Elizabeth glanced back toward the house, planning to call out to the girl. Instead, she gasped, unable to believe her eyes. "Look, Jessica. She's gone!"

Jessica followed Elizabeth's glance. Sure enough, the dark-haired girl was nowhere to be seen. "It happened. Just like the stories say. The Mercandys snatched her right off the sidewalk. Let's get out of here *now*!"

The twins got on their bikes and pedaled away furiously without saying another word. Elizabeth could feel her heart pounding. She didn't really believe that the Mercandy house was haunted, although the stories made Halloween more fun. And she certainly didn't believe that the girl had been snatched right off the sidewalk. Still, she couldn't help wondering who the girl was and just what she was doing at the scariest house in Sweet Valley.

Who is the dark-haired girl and what is the secret of the Mercandy mansion? Find out in **The Haunted House,** *book three in Sweet Valley Twins.*